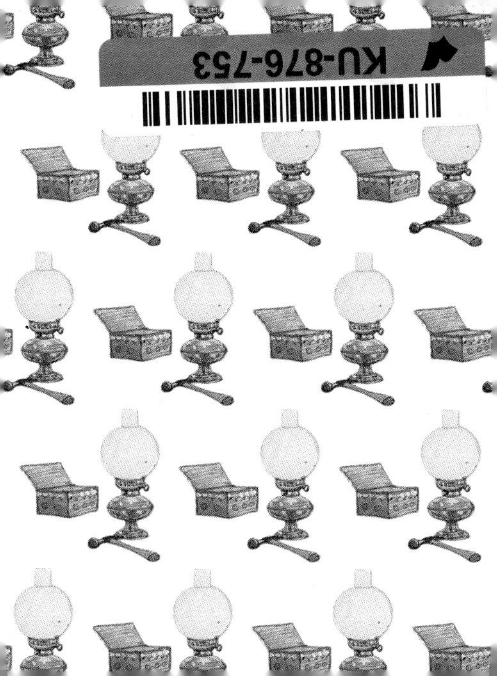

Text copyright © 1976 Mig Holder
Illustrations copyright © 1988 Tony Morris
This edition copyright © 2000 Lion Publishing

The moral rights of the author and illustrator
have been asserted

Published by
Lion Publishing plc
Sandy Lane West, Oxford, England
www.lion-publishing.co.uk
ISBN 0 7459 4559 7

First edition 1976
Second edition 1988
This edition 2000
10 9 8 7 6 5 4 3 2 1 0

Acknowledgments

This story is a retelling of Leo Tolstoy's
adaptation of a story by Ruben Saillens.

A catalogue record for this book is available
from the British Library

Typeset in 11/12.4 Berkeley Oldstyle
Printed and bound in Singapore

Papa Panov's Special Day

Retold by Mig Holder
Illustrations by Tony Morris

LION
Giftlines

A long time ago, almost too long ago to remember, there lived an old shoemaker. His home was far away, almost too far to imagine, in a small Russian village.

His name was Panov. But nobody called him Panov or Mister Panov or even shoemaker Panov; wherever he went in the village he was known as Papa Panov because everybody was so fond of him.

Papa Panov was not very rich – all he owned in the world was one small room looking out onto the village street. And in that one room he lived and slept and made shoes.

But neither was he poor. He always had enough money to buy bread from the baker, coffee from the grocer and cabbage to make soup for his dinner.

So Papa Panov was quite happy – most of the time. Most of the time, his eyes would sparkle through his little round spectacles and he would sing and whistle and shout a cheery greeting to people passing by.

But today it was different.

Papa Panov stood sadly in the window of his little shop and thought of his wife who had died many years before and of his sons and daughters who had all grown up and gone away. It was Christmas Eve and everybody else was at home with their families.

Papa Panov looked up and down the village street and saw windows bright with candles and lamps and Christmas trees. He heard laughter and squeals of children playing games.

Papa Panov sighed a great sigh. Then he slowly lit the oil lamp, went to a high shelf and lifted down an old brown book.

Now Papa Panov had never been to school and could not read very well, so, as he went, he ran his finger along the lines, saying the words out loud.

This was the story of Christmas.
He read how a little boy, Jesus,
was born, not in a warm house
but in a cowshed, because there
wasn't any room at the inn.

'Dearie, dearie,' said Papa Panov,
pulling at his long moustache.
'If they had come here, they
could have slept on my good
bed, and I would have covered
the little boy with my patchwork
quilt.'

He read on, about how the wise
men travelled across the desert to
bring wonderful presents for the
little boy Jesus – presents of gold
and sweet-smelling spices.

'Dearie, dearie,' sighed Papa Panov, 'if Jesus came here, I shouldn't have anything to give him.'

Then he smiled, and his eyes sparkled behind his little round spectacles. He got up from the table and went over to the high shelf. On it was a dusty box tied with string. He opened the box and unwrapped a pair of tiny shoes. Papa Panov held one small shoe in each hand and stood very still. They were the best shoes he had ever made. He put them lovingly away in their box and lowered his old limbs back into the wicker chair.

'That's what I would have given him,' he murmured.

He sighed a deep sigh and, although it was getting late, turned his attention to the book once more.

But it wasn't long before his bony finger slid from the page, his little round spectacles slipped from his nose and he fell sound asleep.

Suddenly, 'Papa, Papa Panov!' said a voice in the room. The old man jumped. His grey moustache quivered.

'Who is it?' he cried, looking about him vaguely. He could see so little without his spectacles, but there seemed to be no one there.

'Papa Panov,' said the voice again. 'You wished that you had seen me, that I had come to your little shop and that you could bring me a gift. Look out into the street from dawn to dusk tomorrow and I will come. Be sure you recognize me, for I shall not say who I am.'

Then all was quiet. Papa Panov rubbed his eyes and sat up with a start. The charcoal in the stove had burned low and the lamp had gone out altogether, but outside, bells were ringing everywhere. Christmas had come.

'It was him,' said the old man to himself. 'That was Jesus.'

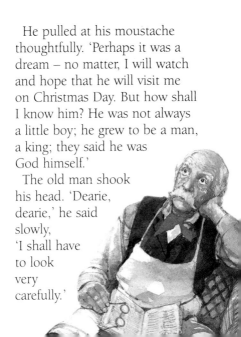

He pulled at his moustache thoughtfully. 'Perhaps it was a dream – no matter, I will watch and hope that he will visit me on Christmas Day. But how shall I know him? He was not always a little boy; he grew to be a man, a king; they said he was God himself.'

The old man shook his head. 'Dearie, dearie,' he said slowly, 'I shall have to look very carefully.'

Papa Panov did not go to bed that night. He sat in his wicker chair, facing the window, and kept watch for the very first person to pass that way. Little by little the sun's rays crept up over the hill and began to brighten the long cobbled street outside.

Nobody was coming yet.

So Papa Panov waited.

At last there was someone: a figure came into view at the far end of the winding road. Papa Panov pressed his face to the frosty glass. He was very excited – perhaps this was Jesus coming to see him. Then he stepped back, disappointed.

The figure was coming closer, trudging slowly up the street. Papa Panov knew who it was – the old roadsweeper who came each week with his barrow and broom.

Papa Panov felt cross. He had better things to do than watch out for an old roadsweeper. He was waiting for God, for the King, Jesus. He turned away from the window impatiently and waited till he thought the old fellow had passed by. But when he turned back, the roadsweeper was there on the other side of the road opposite Papa Panov's shop.

He had set down his barrow and was rubbing his hands together and stamping his feet.

Papa Panov felt sorry. The poor roadsweeper *did* look very cold. And imagine having to work on Christmas Day!

Papa Panov called out from the doorway. 'Hey, old chap!'

The roadsweeper looked round anxiously – people were often very rude to him because of his job – but Papa Panov was smiling.

'How about a cup of coffee?' he called. 'You look frozen to the bone.' The roadsweeper left his barrow at once.

'Don't mind if I do,' he said. 'It's very kind of you, very kind.'

'It's the least I can do,' said Papa Panov, over his shoulder. 'After all, it *is* Christmas.'

The old fellow sniffed. 'Well, this is all the Christmas I'll get.'

Papa Panov returned to his place at the window and gazed up and down the street.

'You expecting visitors?' asked the old roadsweeper gruffly. 'Not in the way, am I?'

Papa Panov shook his head.

'I... Well, have you heard of Jesus?' he asked.

'The Son of God?' asked the old man. 'He's coming today,' replied Papa Panov.

20

The old man looked at him
in astonishment.
So Papa Panov told him
the whole story.
'So that's why I'm
watching out for
him,' he finished
at last.

The roadsweeper set down his mug, shook his head gloomily, and made for the door. 'Well, the best of luck,' he said, 'and thanks for the coffee.' For the first time, the roadsweeper smiled. Then he hurried off into the street, collecting his barrow as he went. Papa Panov stood in the open doorway and watched the roadsweeper disappear.

He was just about to shut the door and go inside when something caught his eye. Stumbling along in the shadows close to the wall was a young woman carrying a baby. She was very thin, her face was tired and her clothes were shabby.

Papa Panov watched her. Suddenly he called out, 'Hello, why don't you come in and warm yourself?' She looked up, startled, and made as if to run away. But she saw the old shoemaker's eyes sparkling behind his spectacles.

'You're very kind,' she said, as he stood aside for her to enter his little shop.

Papa Panov shrugged. 'No, not really,' he said, 'you just looked so cold. Have you got far to go?'

'To the next village,' she replied flatly. 'About four miles. I used to lodge down at the mill, but I have no money left to pay the rent. So I must go and ask my cousin to take me in. I have no husband, you see.'

The woman went inside and stood by the stove. Papa Panov took the baby in his arms. 'Will you share some bread and soup with me?' he asked. But the woman shook her head proudly.

'Well, some milk for the child, then,' he said.

The child chuckled and kicked his feet. 'Dearie, dearie,' said Papa Panov, shaking his head, 'the poor mite has no shoes.'

'I've none to give him,' said the young woman bitterly.

As Papa Panov sat feeding the little boy, a thought came into his mind. He pushed it away – but it came back.

The box from his high shelf! The pair of tiny shoes he had made so long ago – they might fit the baby.

So Papa Panov got them down
from the shelf and tried them
on the child's feet. They fitted
exactly.

'There, you can have these,'
he said softly. The young woman
was overjoyed.

'How can I thank you enough?'
she cried. But Papa Panov didn't
hear. He was looking anxiously
out of the window. Had Jesus gone
by while he was feeding the child?

'Something the matter?' asked
the young woman.

'Have you heard of Jesus who
was born at Christmas?' replied
the old shoemaker. The girl nodded.

'He's coming today,' said Papa Panov, 'he promised.' And he told her all about the dream – if it was a dream.

The young woman listened until he had finished. She looked as if she didn't believe him at all, but she patted the old shoemaker's hand kindly.

'Well, I hope your dream comes true,' she said. 'You deserve it, for being so good to me and the baby.'

And with that she went on her way.

Papa Panov closed the door behind her and, after boiling up a big dish of cabbage soup for his dinner, took his place at the window once again.

Hours ticked by and people came and went. Papa Panov looked closely at everyone who passed. But Jesus did not come.

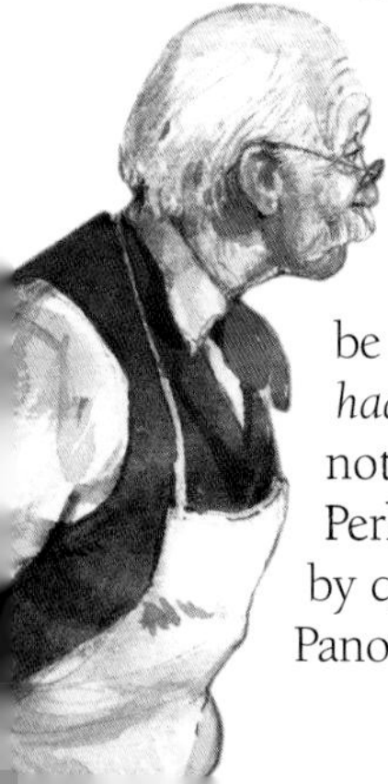

Then he began to be afraid. Perhaps Jesus *had* come, and he had not recognized him. Perhaps he had passed by quickly when Papa Panov had turned away

for a moment. The old shoemaker
could sit still no longer. He went
to the door of the little shop for
one last look.

All sorts of people came by:
children and old men, beggars
and grannies, cheerful people and
grumpy people; to some he gave
a smile, to some a nod and to the
beggars a coin or a hunk of bread.

But Jesus did not come.

As dusk fell, the old shoemaker
sadly lit his oil lamp and took out
his book to read, but his heart was
too heavy and his eyes were too
tired to make out the words on
the page.

'It was only a dream after all,' he said to himself sadly. 'I wanted to believe it so much; I wanted him to come.'

And two great tears welled up behind his spectacles and filled his eyes, so that he could hardly see.

At once it seemed as if there was someone in the room. Through his tears, Papa Panov seemed to see a long line of people passing across the little shop. The roadsweeper was there, and the woman with her child – all the people he had seen and spoken to that day.

And as they passed they whispered, one by one, 'Didn't you see me?

Didn't you see me, Papa Panov?'

'Who are you?' cried the old shoemaker, struggling out of his chair. 'Who are you? Tell me!'

And there came the same voice as the night before, though where it came from, Papa Panov could not have said.

'I was hungry and you gave me food, I was thirsty and you gave me water, I was cold and you took me in.

These people you have helped today – all the time you were helping them, you were helping me!'

Then everything was quiet. The tears dried in the old man's eyes and there was no one to be seen.

'Dearie, dearie,' said Papa Panov slowly, pulling at his long grey moustache. 'So he came after all.'

The old shoemaker shook his head from side to side thoughtfully.

Then he smiled, and the sparkle came back behind his little round spectacles.

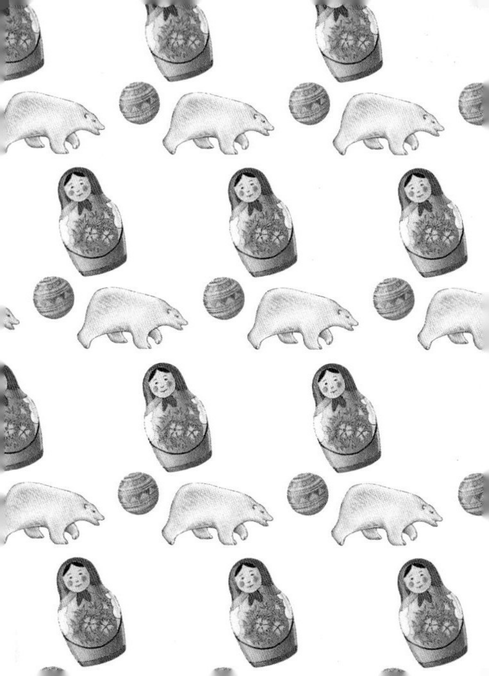

Text copyright © 1982 Arthur Scholey
Illustrations copyright © 1982 Ray and Corinne Burrows
This edition copyright © 2000 Lion Publishing

The moral rights of the author and illustrator
have been asserted

Published by
Lion Publishing plc
Sandy Lane West, Oxford, England
www.lion-publishing.co.uk
ISBN 0 7459 4559 7

First edition 1982
Second edition 1989
This edition 2000
10 9 8 7 6 5 4 3 2 1 0

Acknowledgments

This story is adapted from a broadcast by
BBC Schools Radio; the illustrations are also used
in a Longman/BBC Radiovision filmstrip.

A catalogue record for this book is available
from the British Library

Typeset in 11/12.4 Berkeley Oldstyle
Printed and bound in Singapore

Baboushka

Retold by Arthur Scholey
Illustrations by
Ray and Corinne Burrows

LION
Giftlines

All the villagers were out, bubbling
with excitement.
  'Did you see it again last night?'
  'Of course we did.'
  'Much bigger.'
  'It was moving, coming towards
us. Tonight it will be high above us.'
  That night, excitement, like a
wind, scurried through the lanes
and alleys.
  'There's been a message.'
  'An army is on the way.'
  'Not an army – a procession.'
  'Horses and camels and treasure.'
  Now everyone was itching for
news. No one could work. No one
could stay indoors.

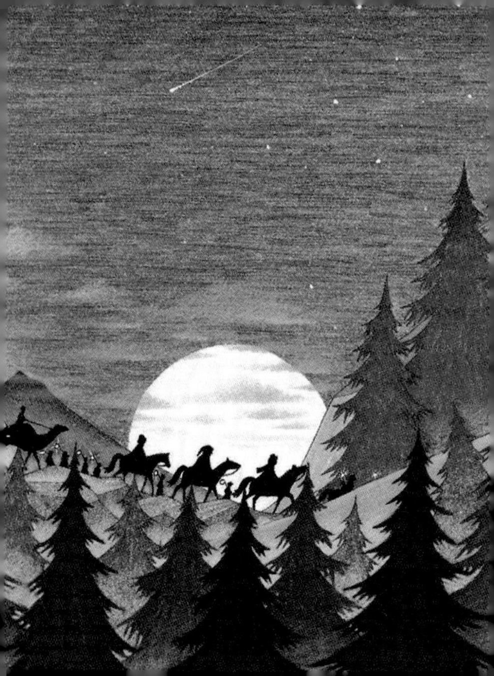

No one, that is, but Baboushka.
Baboushka had work to
do – she always had.
She swept,
polished,
scoured and
shined. Her
house was
the best kept,
best polished,
best washed and
painted. Her
garden was
beautiful,
and her
cooking
superb.

8

'All this fuss for a star!' she muttered. 'I haven't time even to look. I'm so behind, I must work all night!'

So she missed the star at its most dazzling, high overhead. She missed the line of twinkling lights coming towards the village at dawn. She missed the sound of pipes and drums, the tinkling of bells getting louder.

She missed the voices and whispers and then the sudden quiet of the villagers, and the footsteps coming up the path to her door. But the knocking! She couldn't miss that.

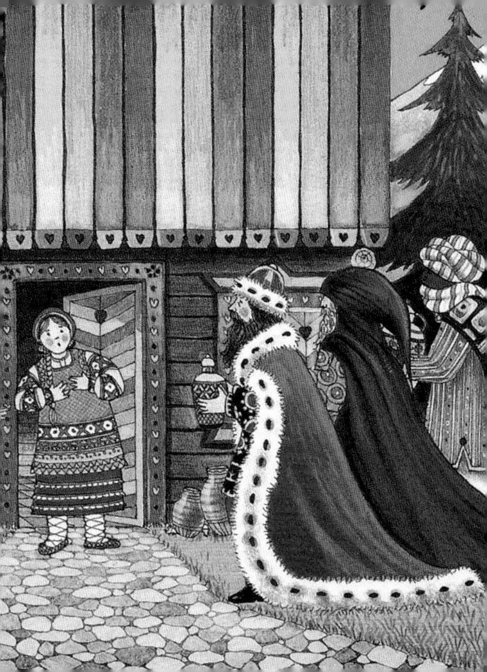

'Now what?' she demanded, opening the door.

Baboushka gaped in astonishment. There were three kings at her door! And a servant.

'My masters seek a place to rest,' he said. 'Yours is the best house in the village.'

'You... want to stay here?'

'It would only be till night falls and the star appears again.'

Baboushka gulped.

'Come in, then,' she said.

How the kings' eyes sparkled at
the sight of the feast Baboushka
set before them.

As she dashed about, serving
them, Baboushka asked question
after question.

'Have you come a
long way?'

'Very far,' sighed
Caspar.

'And where are
you going?'

'We're
following
the star,'
said
Melchior.

'But where?'

They didn't know, they told her. But they believed that it would lead them, in the end, to a newborn king, a king such as the world had never seen before, a king of Earth and Heaven.

'Why don't you come with us?' said Balthasar. 'Bring him a gift as we do. See, I bring gold, and my friends bring spices and ointments.'

'Oh,' said Baboushka. 'I am not sure that he would welcome me. As for a gift...'

'Why, this pickle's fit for any king!' cried Balthasar.

Baboushka laughed. 'Pickle? For a baby? A baby needs toys.' She paused. 'I have a cupboard full of toys,' she said sadly. 'My baby son, my little king, died while very small.'

Balthasar stopped her as she bustled once more to the kitchen.

'This new king could be your king, too. Come with us when the star appears tonight,' he said.

'I'll... I'll think about it,' sighed Baboushka.

15

As the kings slept, Baboushka cleaned and tidied as quietly as she could. What a lot of extra work there was! And this new king. What a funny idea – to go off with the kings to find him. Yet, could she possibly do it? Leave home and go looking for him just like that?

Baboushka shook herself. No time for dreaming! All this washing-up, and putting dishes away, and extra cooking.

Anyway, how
long would
she be away?
What would
she wear?
And what
about gifts?

She sighed.
'There is so much
to do. The house will have to
be cleaned when they've gone.
I couldn't just leave it.'
  Suddenly it was night-time again.
There was the star!
  'Are you ready, Baboushka?'
  'I'll… I'll come tomorrow,'
Baboushka called. 'I'll catch up.
I must just tidy here, find a gift,
get ready…'

18

The kings waved sadly. The star shone ahead. Baboushka ran back into the house, eager to get on with her work.

Sweeping, dusting, beating all the cushions and carpets, cleaning out the kitchen, cooking – away went the night.

At last she went to the small cupboard, opened the door and gazed sadly once again at all those toys. But how dusty they were! One thing was certain. They weren't fit for a baby king. They would all need to be cleaned.

Better get started at once.

On, on, she worked. One by one
the toys glowed, glistened and
gleamed. There! Now they were
fit for the royal baby.

Baboushka looked through the
windows. It was dawn! There was
the sound of the farm cockerel. She
looked up. The star had gone. The
kings would have found
somewhere else to rest
by now. She would
easily catch them up.
At the moment,
though, she felt
so tired. Surely she
could rest now –
just for an hour…

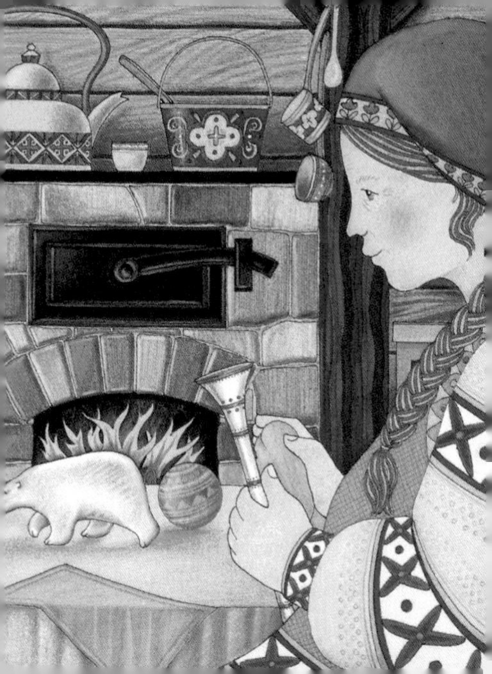

Suddenly, Baboushka was wide awake. It was dark. She had slept all day! She ran out into the street. No star. She rushed back into the house, pulled on her cloak, hurriedly packed the toys in a basket and stumbled down the path the kings had taken.

On she went, hurrying through village after village. Everywhere she asked after the kings.

'Oh yes,' they told her, 'we saw them. They went that way.'

Baboushka lost count of the passing days. The villages grew bigger and became towns. But Baboushka never stopped, night or day. Then she came to a city.

The palace! she thought. That's where the royal baby would be born.

'No royal baby here,' said the palace guard.

'Three kings? What about them?' asked Baboushka.

'Ah yes, they came. But they didn't stay long. They were soon on their way again.'

'But where to?'

'Bethlehem, that was the place.'

I can't imagine why. It's a very poor place. But that's where they went.'
  She set off at once.
  It was evening when Baboushka wearily arrived at Bethlehem.

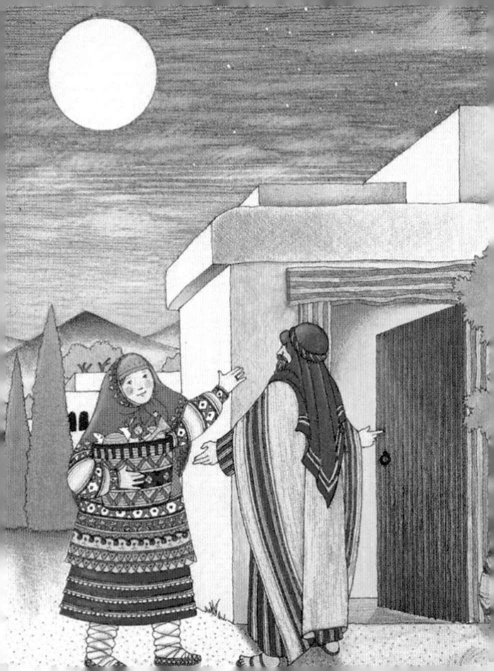

How many days had she been on the journey? She could not remember. And could this really be the place for a royal baby? It didn't look like it. It was not much bigger than her own village. She went to the inn.

'Oh yes,' said the landlord, 'the kings were here two days ago. There was great excitement. But they didn't even stay the night.'

'And a baby?' Baboushka cried. 'Was there a baby?'

'Yes,' said the landlord, 'there was. Those kings asked to see the baby, too.'

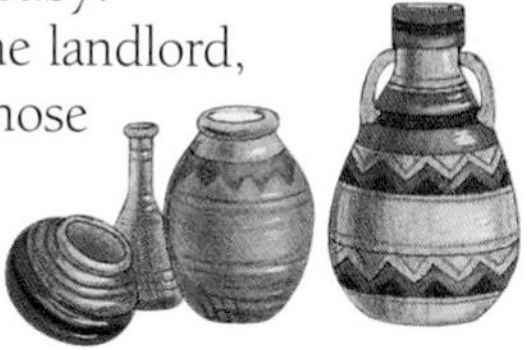

When he saw the disappointment
in Baboushka's eyes, he stopped.

'I'll show you where the baby
was,' he said gently. 'I couldn't
offer the poor couple anything
better at the time. My inn was
packed full. They had to stay in
the stable.'

Baboushka followed him across
the yard.

'Here's the stable,' he said.
Then he left her.

'Baboushka?' came a voice.

Someone was standing in the
half-light of the doorway. He
looked kindly at her. Perhaps he
knew where the family had gone?

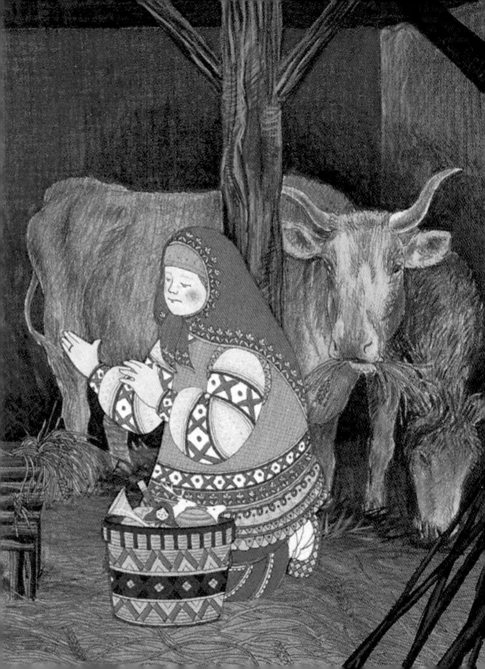

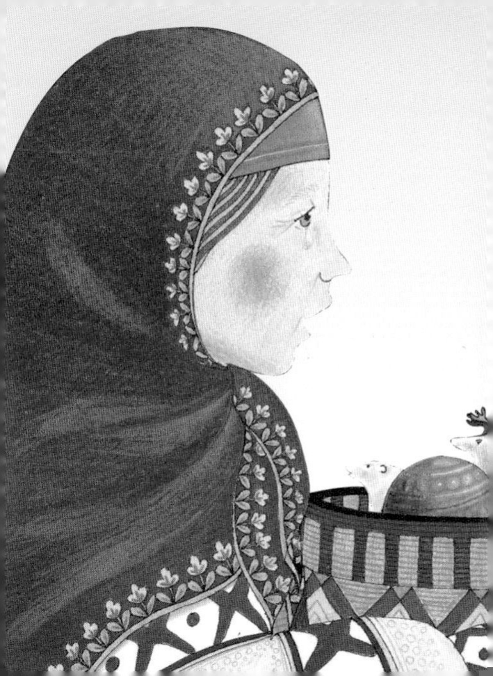

She knew now that the baby king was the most important thing in the world to her.

'They have gone to Egypt, and safety,' he told Baboushka. 'And the kings have returned to their kingdoms. But one of them told me about you. I am sorry, but, as you see, you are too late. Shepherds came as soon as the angels told them.

The kings came as soon as they saw the star. It was Jesus the Christ-child they found, the world's Saviour.'

It is said that Baboushka is still looking for the Christ-child, for time means nothing in the search for things that are real. Year after year she goes from house to house calling, 'Is he here? Is the Christ-child here?'

And at Christmas, when she sees a sleeping child and hears of good deeds, she will lift out a toy from her basket and leave it, just in case.

Then, on Baboushka goes with her journey, still searching, still calling, 'Is he here? Is the Christ-child here?'